Beautiful Grace

A Romancing Marchen Short Story

JENNIFER L. ALLEN

Beautiful Grace
Copyright © 2020 Jennifer L. Allen
All rights reserved.

Published: Jennifer L. Allen 2020
jenniferlallenauthor@gmail.com
Editor: Aimee Lukas
Cover Design: FuriousFotog

In Loving Memory of
Aunt Barbara

Prologue
Grace

Fake plastic snow covered the floor of the high school cafeteria, glittering every time the white and blue lights shone on it. White paper snowflakes hung from the ceiling, occasionally catching that same light. The tables were covered in silvery cloth, and the centerpieces were metallic silver starbursts. Winter wonderland was the theme, and the prom committee had executed it beautifully.

I stood off to the side of the room, watching couples slow dance to yet another Boyz II Men song. I didn't have a date, having chosen to come stag so I wouldn't miss an important milestone in my teenage life...senior prom. My friends didn't have dates either, but when I asked them to come with me, they said they'd rather stay home than show up at prom alone. That kind of thing didn't bother me. I stood out whether I was by myself or in a group. I had spent some of the night chatting with a friend of a friend who had also come alone, but he was in the school's audiovisual club and got roped into helping out with something behind the scenes.

So there I stood. I may have been alone, but I was at my senior prom.

The slow song ended, and couples split up. A techno dance song came on and the girls shrieked and formed little dancing cliques. Their dates watched them in groups from the side of the dancefloor. Occasionally one of the guys would catch sight of me across the way and point, then they and their friends would laugh. It happened periodically throughout the night, girls and guys laughing at me. It had been happening since junior high, and I stopped letting it bother me years ago. "Be the bigger person," my mother had always said.

So that's what I was...always the bigger person. Classmates would whisper and laugh and say things like "Leatherface," "Freddy Kreuger," and the oh-so-original "Scarface." I would ignore their jeers and go about my business. I would kill them with kindness and grace. I would smile when all I really wanted to do was cry. I would never let them see the hurt it caused.

"That's such a pretty dress," someone said, bringing me back to the present. I looked to my left, it was Rosanna Harris. She was one of the most popular girls in my class, and I couldn't believe she was talking to me.

"Thank you," I told her, resisting the urge to twirl and show off the back of the dress. It was a floor length chiffon gown with a cascade ruffle in the back. The one-shoulder design helped hide some of my scars, and the pale pink color didn't drown out my light complexion.

"You look pretty, too," I said, remembering my manners. Rosanna didn't look pretty, though, she looked beautiful. She was in a long, black halter gown with a white ribbon around her tiny waist. Her hair was up in a fancy updo, and she had silver chandelier earrings with what were probably diamonds in them. I'd always envied her straight, white blonde hair. My darker blonde, curly hair always looked messy in comparison.

She laughed lightly. "You're so sweet, Grace," she said. "Always so sweet." The compliment sounded derisive, but she was smiling, so maybe I was imagining things.

The dance song ended, and the class president went up to the podium on the small stage next to the DJ table. My cheeks warmed as J.T. Bell took the mic and cleared his throat. He was so handsome and a genuinely nice guy. He always seemed to look at me, not my scars. Not that we'd interacted all that much over the years. He was one of the popular kids. In fact, he was Rosanna's boyfriend. I thought I heard Rosanna laugh again, but when I peeked at her in my periphery, she was just smiling at J.T..

"Hello, seniors!" J.T. called, earning some wild responses from the crowd. Girls shrieked and guys hooted. Rosanna laughed at the

3

spectacle some players from the football team were making...their end zone dances, maybe? I didn't know, but I was caught up in the excitement, too, laughing along with her and feeling like I belonged there in that cafeteria with my classmates. We were seniors at our senior prom, and this was our last hoorah before graduation. I gave a "woohoo" and clapped with the rest of them, lost in the moment.

J.T. and the class vice president, Katy Jordan, went on to award members of the senior class with various superlatives. Everyone laughed as John Wilson did the worm across the stage to accept his award. He was aptly named class clown, and the slideshow showed an image of him from his ventriloquist skit at the school's talent show. J.T. blushed when he was awarded class heartthrob. A few more awards were handed out for most likely to succeed, best car, and best smile.

"And now for the moment we've all been waiting for...prom king and queen," J.T. said.

"Oh, J.T.," Katy Jordan cooed. "You missed one." She handed him an envelope and he frowned. They exchanged a few words, but their mics were down so no one could hear what they were saying.

J.T. shrugged and lifted his mic. "Looks like we've got one more category for you tonight," he said as he opened the envelope. "The winner of most...*unique*...is," he flipped over the card just as Katy Jordan pressed the button on the slideshow remote to move to the next picture.

My yearbook picture stared back at me and the rest of the senior class. My face was angled just so and my hair set just right so that my scars were mostly covered. Of course, it was impossible to completely cover the right side of my face.

"Grace Adams," J.T. said, his voice echoing in the sudden quiet. He sounded as confused as I felt.

That hadn't been a category we'd voted on the week before when we received the ballots for class superlatives. This had to be a joke, right? A sick, stupid joke. Most unique? Well, yeah. The girl with the scars on her face from a freak motorcycle accident had to be the most unique in the senior class.

No one said a word, but they all turned to look at me.

"Go on up," Rosanna said in her saccharine sweet voice. She even gave me a little push.

I glanced at her. The smile she wore that I'd only partially seen before was as derisive as her tone had been. I wanted to tell her to fuck off. I wanted to tell them all to fuck off. But I wouldn't. I would ignore them. I would kill them with kindness and grace. I would smile and push my way through this situation like I pushed my way through every other embarrassing situation I'd experienced since gaining my scars.

5

I pasted on my brightest smile, fake as it was, and kept my chin up and my back straight as I left Rosanna's side and made my way to the stage. J.T. looked uncomfortable and Katy looked pleased with herself as she tapped the rolled piece of paper against her free hand. She smirked as she handed it to me and then took two steps back. I turned to face the senior class, my cheeks--well, cheek--on fire but my smile still firmly in place. They all looked so elegant and classy in their formal dress. They looked like anything but what they actually were...immature children.

No one said anything as my eyes scanned the crowd, smile still firmly in place. I must have either looked like I was happy to be considered for an award or like I was a little crazy. I didn't know, I just knew I wasn't going to let them see me break.

As I took a step forward to move off the stage, I was hit with something from out in the crowd. It hit my right shoulder and burst. I looked down and my pretty pink dress was stained red. There was what looked like a broken latex balloon on the floor by my feet.

What the hell?

I looked up, expecting to see the culprit, but I only saw my classmates looking at me. Pointing and whispering.

Another hit, this time on the left. Another one, then another one. One hit my forehead, the dyed water running into my eyes. I held up my hands to guard my face, but one after another after another came at me. I wanted to run but I was frozen in place. Where were the teachers? The chaperones?

People were laughing now. I couldn't see because whatever they used to dye the water stung my eyes. I didn't know where the balloons were coming from and which direction I needed to block. I tried to move out of the way, but I didn't know where to go. I was frozen in place, pelted with balloon after balloon. The small water bombs stung as they pinged off my skin. I took a step to the side in a meager effort to escape and tripped, falling to my knees. Pain shot through my legs and I cried out. Rolling to my side, I pulled my knees into my chest as my classmates continued to pelt me. With my face tucked away, I cried.

Their laughter and woots...the sound of their fun...haunted me for a very, very long time.

Chapter 1
Grace

My eyes blinked open, catching sight of the ceiling fan. The rotations of the blades were much like my life lately. Spinning, spinning, spinning. At least it felt that way, punctuated by last night's dream.

That dream was different, though. Usually when I dreamt about that night, I imagined myself walking off the makeshift stage with my head held high, red dye be damned. A final fuck-you to the senior class for trying to humiliate me, yet again, for my differences.

My *unique*ness.

Last night's dream was, well, it was how it really happened. I'd lost all the bravado I'd ever had and cried on the floor of the stage like a baby. I'd reached the end of my rope. Who could blame me? That might also be the reason for the third version of that dream...the one where I went all Stephen King's Carrie on them...fires and explosions everywhere.

I knew it all had to do with the fact that after ten years away, I'd finally returned to the small town of Marchen. It was the last place I'd expected to take my library science degree, but when the librarian position at the elementary school had become available at the same time my mother got sick, I saw it as a sign.

I sighed, getting up from my bed. Today was the first day of school and despite the dream, I was looking forward to it. I couldn't wait to meet the kids. I'd always wanted to work in an elementary school, and I spent the last four years biding my time as an assistant librarian in a collegiate library at a small Christian university. I'd miss a handful of my coworkers, but I was more than ready for the change.

I zipped through my morning routine and dressed in the outfit I'd laid out for myself the night before: a black pencil skirt and a soft purple sweater vest over a white button down. I never wore a lot of makeup, choosing only to dust on a little blush, mascara, and a dark lip gloss. My wavy blonde hair was swept back into a loose, low bun.

I stared at my reflection in the bathroom mirror. If I hadn't worn them for years, I'd never have known I'd once had scars marring the right side of my face, shoulder, and arm. The plastic surgeon had done wonders to erase the evidence of the accident from my skin.

I blotted my lips and flipped off the light without another glance at the familiar stranger in the mirror.

Maybe one day I'd get used to her.

I reached for my favorite heels, then opted for the black patent leather flats instead, knowing I'd be on my feet most of the day as the kindergarten classes took turns coming to the library. My predecessor had told me that first through third grades were often self-sufficient, only requesting help finding items occasionally, but the kindergarteners were an entirely hands-on bunch. I was looking forward to it.

A few hours later, the only thing I was looking forward to was my lunch break. The little ones, adorable as could be, were like tiny tornadoes. I'd reset shelves and displays in between classes three times before giving up. I made a mental note to create some rules that included cleaning up after themselves. Little kids loved to have jobs, I hoped.

Kindergarten ate lunch in the cafeteria at 10:30, and since I wasn't expecting students from any other grades, I took advantage of that opportunity to eat my lunch. There was a teachers' lounge near the main office, but I wasn't feeling very social. I needed time to decompress, and there was no better place to do that than a quiet library.

I took the brown paper sack out of my tote bag and carried it to the back corner of the library where the biographies were located. When I'd been a student at Marchen Elementary, the nonfiction section was always the quietest. I'd often taken my favorite storybook to that corner and gotten lost in the tales.

I sat down on the worn carpet, my legs stretched out in front of me, and began unpacking my lunch bag. Once I had everything laid out, I started picking at my food and thinking about my morning. It was wild, but the joy on those little faces when they saw their favorite character on a book cover was unforgettable.

A giggle had me looking up from my makeshift picnic. Standing at the end of the row was a small, brown haired little girl. She looked too big to be a kindergartener, but I could have been wrong.

"Well, hello there," I called over to her. She giggled again, then she shushed me. I smiled, tucking my legs beside me so I could get to my feet gracefully. "I think *I'm* the one who is supposed to say that," I said, walking down the aisle. "I'm the librarian."

Her wide eyes looked up at me as I approached. "You look like a princess," she said. "Rapunzel."

"And you are incredibly sweet to say so," I told her, feeling the weight of my long hair on my back. It must have come loose from its bun in all my shuffling around this morning. When I reached the end of the aisle, I noticed there was no one else with the little girl. "Where's your class, hon?"

She frowned. "Ms. Murphy sent me down."

I fought the urge to frown with her. Ms. Murphy had been teaching third grade when *I* was in elementary school. The woman was nasty when I had her, I could only imagine how she was twenty years later.

I bent my knees, lowering myself to my new friend's level--because, let's face it, if she thought I look like a princess then she was definitely my friend.

"Do you need help finding a book?" I asked.

Still frowning, she said "My dad forgot to put my book in my backpack this morning."

"Oh no," I said, making a sad face and being sure to stick my lower lip out in an exaggerated pout of solidarity. "Silly daddy. Do you have a new book in mind, or did you want to see if we have the same book?"

Her dark eyes lit up. "Let's see if you have the same book!"

I laughed, enjoying her enthusiasm. *That* was why I wanted to be a school librarian. I loved the energy that rolled off of kids who were excited about books and reading.

"What's the name of the book?"

She rattled off the title and then began telling me about the book. I walked around the front desk and began typing the title into the search field on the computer.

"Looks like we have what you're looking for," I told her, and her eyes sparkled. "Come with me." I led her to the appropriate area of the library, explaining to her how she could find books using the computer.

"I think my class is coming to the library on Thursdays," she said. "Most of the kids probably already know their way around the library but I'm brand new."

I lowered myself to her level again and smiled. "Do you want to know a secret?" I asked. She grinned and nodded. "I'm brand new, too. Today is my first day."

Her eyes widened. "It's *my* first day, too."

I stuck out my pinky and she wrapped hers around it. "Then I guess we'll just have to look out for each other, won't we?"

She nodded, her expression very serious. "Will you be my friend? I haven't made any yet."

"I would love to be your friend. Now let's get you all checked out and back to your class." We returned to the front desk and I went behind the counter to the computer. "What's your name?"

"Abigail Bell."

I froze for a moment, but only for a moment. There was *no way* she could be related to J.T.

Bell. That would have been too crazy of a coincidence. I eyed the little girl as I typed her name in the computer and scanned the book. Her hair was darker than J.T.'s had been, and her eyes were lighter. Bell was a common enough last name, right? An awful coincidence for there to be a different Bell family in Marchen, though. Did J.T. have a brother? I didn't remember one.

"Here you go, Abigail."

"My friends call me Abby," she said, taking the book from me.

"It was nice to meet you, Abby. I'll see you on Thursday." I winked and she winked back, seemingly thrilled to be part of a little secret.

I watched her as she walked to the squeaky swinging doors of the library. She turned and waved at me once more before pushing her way through.

What a sweet kid, I thought as the doors swung shut behind her. Could she be J.T.'s daughter? Abby had said she was new...was it possible that J.T. and I had both returned to Marchen at the same time? My mind was running away from me. There was a myriad of possibilities, and J.T.'s involvement was only one of them. I was only fixated on him because I'd had the dream. That was all.

"Knock, knock!" a woman said, pushing through the doors with an impressively straight line of tiny humans behind her.

I focused on the present and greeted the new class of kindergarteners and their teacher.

Chapter 2
Jonah

"How was school?" I asked Abby as she met me in a grassy area outside the school. The parent pick-up spot was by a large oak tree on the side of the elementary school campus.

"It was okay," she said, not looking at me.

She'd gotten her attitude from her mother and was still mad at me for moving us away from her friends and back to *my* hometown, emphasis on the "my." She had way too much attitude for an eight-year-old, and with every day that passed, I resented Allison a little more for leaving us. Then I felt horribly guilty for even thinking that. Allison hadn't wanted to go, even though she'd been more than ready when the time came.

"Just okay?" I asked, hoping to get a little more out of her.

She just shrugged, shuffling her feet and looking around. There was an assortment of mothers and fathers greeting their kids in the parent pick-up area, and I noticed Abby's gaze stay on the mothers a little longer.

I ran my hand over my hair in frustration. I had a lot I still needed to learn. I didn't know how to be a dad *and* a mom. Maybe that was something my mom could teach me now that I was back home. Allison had been great at the whole mom thing. She knew the right way to kiss boo-boos and how to make the best peanut butter and fluff sandwiches. I didn't even know what fluff was until my eight-year-old told me. Forget the boo-boos. Abby's first little scrape after Allison passed resulted in her crying herself to sleep because I couldn't console her. I'd felt like shit that night, camped out on her bedroom floor, unable to make it better because I couldn't bring her mom back. Every day got a little better, but there were still moments when I felt like an epic failure. I supposed there always would be.

"How about we go out to dinner tonight to celebrate the end of the first day of school?" No response. "We can have ice cream for dessert."

Abby looked up. "Can I get a strawberry milkshake?"

"You can have whatever you want," I said, promising myself I would not make it a habit to spoil my child.

"Okay," she said. Then she took my hand and began to walk, and I wondered...had I just been had?

"I would like the grilled cheese and some french fries," Abby ordered.

Our waitress, a tall, skinny redhead with a name tag that read "Becky," smiled at Abby as she wrote her order down. "Sure thing." I was sure she was related to an old classmate of mine, James Howard, who had also been tall and skinny and had equally red hair. I thought I remembered he'd had a younger sister. There wasn't much change in a small town like

Marchen, so I didn't imagine there were too many new people.

"How about some veggies, Abs?" My daughter glared at me. "Grilled cheese and french fries it is," I said. Allison had her ways of getting Abby to eat vegetables. Add that to the list of things I'd need to learn to do. "I'll have the meatloaf special," I told Becky.

"I'll have those right out," Becky said, stepping away from the table.

We sat across from each other at a large booth in the Marchen Diner. She went straight to her room after school and didn't come out until I called her for dinner. She was eight going on eighteen and I was in more trouble than I wanted to admit. My job as a data analyst allowed me to work from home so I could have flexible hours and be there for Abby, whether she wanted me there or not--often it was the latter.

"Do you want to tell me more about school?" I asked Abby.

She twisted her lips, something her mother always did when she was thinking about something. "You forgot my book."

Ah-ha. That was probably why she was mad at me. I saw her book on her nightstand when I went to take her laundry basket to be washed and wondered if she'd needed that.

"The book you left on your nightstand?" I asked. Her eyes narrowed at me, but I didn't give in. I had to put my foot down sometime. Abby had always liked having responsibilities, so I thought that was a good angle. "Hasn't it always been your responsibility to pack your backpack?"

She sighed. *Jesus.* Eight going on eighteen for sure. "Yes," she finally said.

"So who *really* forgot your book?"

"I did," she said, and the words sounded like they weighed two hundred pounds as they left her little mouth.

"Did you get in trouble in class?"

She shrugged. "Mrs. Murphy sent me to the library."

Mrs. Murphy. The woman was ancient when I was in elementary school. I couldn't believe it when I saw her name on Abby's registration forms. Marchen Elementary had two third grade classes now, versus the one when I was Abby's age. It was just my luck my daughter would have the same teacher as me. I just couldn't believe Mrs. Murphy was still teaching.

"Did the library have the book?"

My little girl's eyes lit up and my heart warmed, her eyes hadn't lit up like that enough in the last four years.

"The librarian looks like a princess. She has really long hair like Rapunzel. She's really nice, too. Today was her first day of school, too." Abby frowned. "That was supposed to be a secret. Don't tell her I told you, okay?"

I doubted I would be meeting the school librarian, so I figured that was a secret I could keep. "Deal. I'm glad she was nice to you."

"She was so nice and so pretty." She sipped her chocolate milk through the straw then her eyes widened. "There she is, Daddy!"

I looked in the direction Abby was pointing and saw a woman walk in the diner. She looked to be about my age and "pretty" didn't quite describe her. She was beautiful. Her blonde hair was twisted into a messy bun on top of her head and she wore gray leggings and a dark green sweater. She was smiling at something the hostess was saying, then she was grinning down at a little girl...at *my* little girl.

I stupidly glanced across the table where my daughter had been sitting, knowing the spot would be empty because my daughter was talking to the beautiful stranger by the door.

I got up from the booth and met them at the front of the diner. "I'm sorry, it seems my daughter is quite taken by the new librarian who looks a lot like Rapunzel."

The librarian looked up at me from where she was kneeling in front of Abby and when her eyes locked on mine, she seemed to freeze in place. She stood abruptly and looked towards a booth along the wall where a woman sat wearing a similar outfit but with a knit cap over her head. Odd, since the weather hadn't yet turned cold in our southern town.

"It was good to see you, Abby. I'll see you on Thursday." She smiled politely at my daughter, but it was not nearly as bright as it had been before I joined them. She hurried away, sparing me no second glance, and Abby and I were left standing alone at the door.

"Was it something I said?" I asked.

Abby sighed, then returned to the table.

I sighed, too, then followed her.

Chapter 3
Grace

Thursday came entirely too soon, and Mrs. Murphy's class was due to walk through the library doors any minute. I was terrified at the arrival one student.

Abigail Bell's father was J.T. Bell. The most attractive guy I'd ever known growing up and one of *them*. He'd deceived me so well in high school. Acting kind and oblivious to the bullying. Boy had I been wrong. He looked different now, older obviously, with a beard and long dark blonde hair. He looked like a lumberjack. A sexy lumberjack. When my eyes met his at the diner, I thought I'd drop dead then and there. I felt all the mortification I'd felt at senior prom. I'd wanted to go straight home, but my mom was having a good day, and I didn't want to spoil that for her. It didn't seem like J.T. knew who I was; how could he considering I could no longer be recognized as the girl voted most unique in our senior class? I pulled a protective bubble over my table at the diner and stayed inside it. I didn't look their way. I didn't even look at the server when I ordered. I'd been so rude, but I had entered self-preservation mode, and I wasn't very thoughtful of others when I was in it.

I knew it was bound to happen, though. I wouldn't be able to sneak around our small town without anyone knowing I was there for long. I was certain the Marchen gossip chain had shared my arrival when I'd driven into town trailing a small U-Haul behind my car. I wondered why I hadn't heard anything about J.T. though. Regardless, I was sure I'd run into other classmates from Marchen High eventually.

The library doors swung open, and Mrs. Murphy walked in, her class following behind.

"Grace," she said, acknowledging me. I wasn't sure if she'd been debriefed on the new librarian or if she recognized me. I wouldn't put it past her to know who I was by sight. She was one of those older women in town who always seemed to know everything. She'd probably originated the Marchen gossip train. Why wouldn't she know that I'd gotten plastic surgery? Most of the school faculty knew about my surgery since I'd been homeschooled for the rest of my senior year because of it.

"Mrs. Murphy," I said. "It's good to see you."

"Likewise," she said, and I think she may have smiled, too, if that twitch at the side of her mouth was any indication. Could have just been a twitch, though.

I went through an abbreviated version of my library orientation since most of these students had already been through a more comprehensive orientation in earlier grades. The class split up and disappeared into the stacks to find their books. Abby stayed by me, holding the book she'd checked out on Monday and looking sad.

"Hi, Abby," I said, approaching her. "Is everything okay? Do you need help finding something?" She shook her head, and I wasn't sure which question she was responding to. I kneeled in front of her and looked into her big brown eyes. "What's the matter, sweetie?"

"I already checked out a book this week so I can't pick a new one. Mrs. Murphy said so."

That witch.

I frowned. "I'm sorry, Abby. Is that your class rule?"

She nodded, her eyes filling with tears. I wanted to break that class rule for her, but I knew better than to undermine a teacher my first week of school, particularly one that had tenure and was probably as old as the school itself.

"There's a really neat library in the next town over. Maybe this weekend your Mom and Dad can take you there to check out a few books."

Two big tears spilled down her cheeks.

Shit.

What did I say?

"My Mom is in heaven. Do they ha-have libraries in heaven?"

Shit. Shit. Shit.

I carefully thought about how to reply. "I think heaven has a huge library. I bet your Mom can read any book she wants, when she's not looking down on you."

Abby wiped her tears away with small fists, her expression turning hopeful. "You think so?"

"I know so," I said, nodding. "It's one of the first things we learn in librarian school."

Abby smiled and hugged the book she was holding against her chest. "I remembered my book from home, so I can return this one."

"That's okay," I said, winking at her. "You can hold on to it to read it while you're here. You can give it back to me before you go."

Her eyes sparkled. "Thank you, Princess Librarian," she giggled.

"You can call me Miss Adams."

"I like Princess Librarian better."

I laughed. "Yeah, me too."

"Do you know anything about J.T. Bell?" I asked my mom.

She tilted her head to the side. "The name sounds familiar, but I'm not entirely sure why."

The chemotherapy Mom was receiving to treat her breast cancer was doing its job, but it was wreaking havoc on her memory and thought processing. Sometimes she would forget something she'd known her whole life and other times she couldn't complete a sentence. The next minute she was just as witty as she'd always been. It was a wild ride.

"He's just someone I went to high school with." I said, trying to downplay my curiosity.

"Jonah!" Mom said, causing me to jump. I nearly cut the tip of my finger off instead of the carrot I'd been chopping for tonight's beef stew. Mom was craving it, and she doesn't crave much so I'm all about indulging her.

"What?"

"Jonah Bell. That's his name. He went by J.T. in high school, but his name is Jonah. Shame what happened to his wife. Poor boy, and their daughter."

"What happened to his wife?" I asked; I already knew she had passed, but I didn't know what had happened.

"Leukemia. She had it as a child, and I guess it came back some years ago. Everything happened so quickly, poor thing didn't have a chance."

Cancer. Why was it always cancer? It seemed that everyone had their own cancer story. When I had told my co-workers I'd be leaving the university to go home and be with my mom, they all had their own stories to share. The ones that resulted in death were hard to hear. I knew they meant well, but I wish they'd been more careful with their retellings. My mom's chances were good, but it was still cancer, so anything was possible as far as I was concerned.

"Did you ever meet her?" My mom had spoken of her like she was familiar, maybe J.T. and his wife had lived in Marchen at some point. Maybe his wife had been one of our classmates.

"No, but Deirdre Bell is part of my ladies bible study group. She spoke of her often, made me feel like I knew her. Left behind a little girl, so sad."

I couldn't argue with that. Abby seemed to still be healing from her mother's death. But honestly, did a little girl ever truly heal from her mother's death? I didn't want to think about it.

"Abby, the daughter, goes to my school."

Mom nodded. "I think I remember Deirdre say they were moving home. She'd asked Jonah all the time. Wanted to help. I don't remember the daughter-in-law's name, but I don't think she had any family. They lived out in California or something and poor Jonah was all by himself."

I didn't want to feel bad for him, but I was starting to. It must have been difficult for him to lose his wife and have to raise Abby by himself. Poor Jonah, indeed. Then I remembered prom night.

Screw Jonah.

Abby was a sweet little girl, and I would never hold her responsible for the sins of her father, but I didn't have to like him. Or feel sympathy for him.

"Why are you asking about Jonah?" Mom asked, and even though I'd just told her, I'd tell her again.

I'd always tell her again.

Chemo brain be damned.

Chapter 4
Jonah

Three weeks into the school year was marked with parents' night. Each grade appeared to have a theme and the third-grade theme was math. Poor kids. Kindergarten had art; that looked like a lot of fun. Messy, but fun.

Abby had the best time showing me some of the math problems she could complete using colored blocks. She smiled brightly, and I was so proud of her in that moment. Kids still loved school and learning in third grade, and that was apparent on my daughter's face.

I'd be lying if I said I wasn't curious about the librarian. I wondered if parents' night made its way to the library at all. I was attracted to her--who wouldn't be? She was gorgeous. A princess, even. More than that, I was intrigued. Abby told me how *Princess Librarian* had told her heaven had all the books and that Allison was probably reading whatever she wanted whenever she wasn't with Abby. Every night since, when I'd tuck Abby into bed, she asked me what I thought Mommy was reading. It broke my heart and warmed it at the same time. I wanted to see this librarian princess again so I could thank her. Abby had reached some level of peace since meeting her. I had no idea if it would stick, but I appreciated the reprieve from my tiny teenager-to-be all the same.

"Did you hear me, Daddy?" Abby asked, smacking her little hand against my arm.

"No, what?"

She rolled her eyes dramatically. "I *said,* we're doing a performance in the auditorium."

Abby and her class went backstage while I followed the rest of the parents into the auditorium. A few people openly stared at me, while others did it more subtly. In a small town like Marchen, I was sure everyone already knew my life story, but they hadn't seen me yet. I supposed I stuck out like a sore thumb in an elementary school with my beard and my long hair.

Ask me if I cared, though. I'd stopped cutting my hair somewhere around the time Allison got sick. She'd always given me haircuts, and it never felt right going to anyone else.

I took a seat in the back row, away from prying eyes, and kept my eyes on the stage. The room filled up as I sat there, and I caught a flash of blonde hair to my left. I looked over and saw *her.* Without thinking, I stood from my seat and side-stepped down the row, saying "excuse me" as I stepped over people. I took the seat beside her.

"Hello," I said, smiling. "We didn't get to talk when we met at the diner. My daughter, Abby, speaks very highly of you. I wanted to introduce myself. My name is Jonah Bell," I said, offering my hand.

She glared back at me. "I know who you are," she said firmly, not taking my hand. She was angry with me, and I didn't know why.

26

"Well, you have me at a disadvantage. You know me, but I don't know you." I tilted my head to the side, taking her in. She looked vaguely familiar--her eyes, in particular--but I couldn't place her.

"Leigh Adams," she said, still glaring at me. Then she stood from her seat and hurried away.

I watched her go, unsure as to what had just happened. She clearly didn't like me. Was it something Abby had told her? Abby was into her stories, but she wasn't very theatrical. I couldn't imagine she'd share something with her librarian that wasn't true.

Leigh.

Her name didn't sound familiar. I didn't remember anyone with the name Leigh. There was a girl in my class with the last name Adams, but the librarian was not her. I would have recognized Grace Adams. She was one of the kindest girls in my class before she left school. The prank our classmates pulled on her during prom was rotten. I'd broken up with Rosanna that night because of her part in it. I had wondered what ever happened to Grace, but I hadn't known her well enough to find out.

The lights dimmed and the curtain parted. There were risers set up on the stage and it looked like all the elementary students stood on them. I spotted Abby in the fourth row and waved, even though I doubted she could see me. The kids started singing a song about the states and eventually parents started clapping along. I went through the motions, but my mind was still on the librarian.

Who was she and why did she dislike me so much?

Chapter 5
Grace

"Hi, my name is Jonah. My daughter likes you. Want to be friends?" I muttered in a terrible, goofy version of his voice. I folded a pair of pants and slammed them onto my bed before moving on to a t-shirt.

Jonah.

I couldn't believe he had the audacity to sit next to me in the auditorium. Like he was my friend. Of course, he wouldn't recognize me with my new face. He had no idea who I was. I wasn't sure why I gave him my middle name, though. I had nothing to hide. He was the one who should be ashamed, not me. The only reason I could come up with for my little mistruth was that I wasn't ready for the confrontation my true identity would have brought. If he knew who I was, he'd probably ask about my face. He might even try to apologize for the way he treated me in high school. "It was so long ago," he'd say. "I've grown up." Blah blah blah.

I had to admit though, he was still so dreamy. The long hair and beard were different, but he wore it well. He'd aged nicely over the last ten years. Definitely took care of himself. My third day back in town I'd seen Jeremy Owens, one of the other popular guys in our class. He'd hit on me at the Gas and Grind where he worked as a mechanic. I was ordering a much-needed coffee at the "Grind" part of the establishment and Charlotte Peppermill, the barista who had been a class behind ours, told him to buzz off. The years had *not* been kind to Jeremy. He'd probably gained fifty pounds, mostly around the middle, and was very...greasy...his job as an auto mechanic did not seem to be the cause.

"Gracie," Mom called from down the hall. I was staying with her in the main house for the duration of her treatment. My plan was to move to the apartment over the garage when she was well enough to take care of herself again.

My parents had never been married, but my father took excellent--financial--care of my mother. He could afford to. My mother was an independently published mystery writer. She kept her career low-key and made just enough to keep her comfortable and make a nice savings for herself in case the day came when my dad could no longer pay her way. But she didn't have health insurance, and my father stepped in in a big way when it came to her cancer treatments. It wasn't cheap.

"Coming," I called. I finished folding my shirt and set it down on top of the pants. The rest would have to wait. Mom was in the sick part of her chemo cycle, so she was my priority. "Can I get you something?" I asked as I entered the living room where she was laying on the couch.

"I'd like to try some chicken soup."

I smiled, "Coming right up." I was always pleased when she tried to eat. For some reason she seemed to enjoy super salty foods, and I wouldn't complain as long as she was eating something.

I went to the kitchen and took a can of chicken noodle soup out of the cupboard, opened it and poured it into the small saucepan that was cleaned and waiting on the stove. I turned the burner on and went to sit next to my mom on the couch.

"Hear from your dad?" she asked. Even though they weren't together, I knew my mom loved my dad. He loved her, too. Once I was born, they decided it was best for me and my mom to live together apart from my father. It would keep us both safe, and that's what my dad wanted most. His lifestyle was too...wild...for the kind of life he wanted his daughter to have.

"He called a few days ago." He called me once a week to check in, I saw him much less frequently.

"What's he up to?"

I shrugged. I didn't know what my dad was up to because he didn't share that kind of thing with me, and I was perfectly okay with that. He was into dangerous stuff, and all I really cared about was that he called. It meant he was alive, and I could sleep easy for another week.

Mom didn't ask anything else. She knew the drill. She was with my dad, deeply engaged in his crazy life for three years before she got pregnant. I was a game changer for her, for both of them. Seeing my mom decked out in mom jeans and bedazzled shirts makes me wonder how she ever fit into my dad's world, but that was probably part of the ruse. She was a rebel within.

I got up to check the soup, transferred it to a bowl, and placed it on a tray with some cucumber water and crackers. I brought it out to the living room and set it on the coffee table, then I helped Mom to sit up.

"You good here? I'm going to finish my laundry."

"Yes. Thank you, Gracie."

"Of course. Holler if you need anything."

If you thought I'd be sick of the library after spending five days a week in one, you'd be wrong. I loved the library, particularly the big library in Gaston, one town over. I spent a few hours every Sunday getting lost in some of the old volumes they had in their preservation room. It was a museum of sorts, filled with leather-bound editions of classic novels.

I picked up a copy of *Gone with the Wind*, carefully opening the cover to see the publication date of that particular edition, when a voice startled me.

"Fancy meeting you here," he whispered over my right shoulder. His breath tickled as it moved across my new skin.

I sucked in a breath, nearly dropping the book. I checked to make sure I hadn't torn it before I acknowledged him.

Why was he everywhere?

I carefully returned the book to its place on the shelf and turned to him. "Do you mind?" I whisper-hissed at him. It *was* a library after all.

He shrugged, a sly smile spreading across his face. He was so handsome, and he smelled so good, like peppermint and something woodsy. It was hard to resist his charm, but I would.

"It seems Princess Librarian told Abby about this library the first week of school and we've been here every weekend since," he said, looking around at the shelves filled with old books. "What is this place?"

"It's the preservation room. Old books," I added simply.

"Hm," his gaze shifted back to me. "I saw you in here and thought I'd come say hi," he said, gesturing to the glass wall between this room and the main library.

"I'm not sure why you thought that was a good idea."

He laughed softly. "I'm not sure either. I get the feeling you don't like me."

"You'd be correct," I said smartly. "Want a prize?"

"No, but I'd love to know why. I just met you, Leigh."

"That's not my name," I snapped, getting more irritated by the minute. It pissed me off that he didn't know who I was. I understood that he wouldn't recognize me because of my surgery, but some irrational part of me felt like he should know by default. The other side of my face was still the same. Had he not spent any time in high school looking at that? Had he always focused on the scars? It should be a rule. When you ruined someone's life, you never forgot them.

"But you said..."

"I know what I said. I lied. My name is Grace. Grace Adams." I pushed past him quickly and went through the door, leaving him standing in the preservation room with his mouth wide open.

Chapter 6
Jonah

I wanted to run after her, but I didn't. I just stood there like a gaping fool.

She *was* Grace Adams.

Damn, she looked so different. I never would have guessed Princess Librarian was Grace, the girl from high school with the scars who was teased mercilessly. She'd always handled it with such grace, though. I'd admired that about her. There were times I succumbed to peer pressure--who didn't?--and when I was regretting whatever it was my friends got me to do, I often thought about Grace and how she'd never allow herself to be pressured in that way. I thought about her occasionally over the years, but I never would have reached out to her because I wouldn't have known what to say. As it was, she'd been right in front of me and I didn't know what to say.

I left the weird glass room full of musty old books and looked for Abby in the children's section. There was an older lady reading to a group of kids, and Abby was sitting on the edge of the group, engrossed in the story. My daughter was such a bookworm, she got it from her mom. I hoped that one day I'd be able to tell a story as good as her mom could. I was a work in progress in that area, something Abby wasn't afraid to tell me at bedtime.

I leaned against the wall near a bulletin board, waiting for story time to finish. There was an October calendar pinned to the board and my eyes scanned it for something Abby might like. Something entirely different caught my eye, though. A fundraiser for the library's preservation room. It said to "dress appropriately," and there was a historical theme. My mind's eye immediately went to Grace in a gown like the ladies wore in the old movies. She certainly had the body for it.

I shook my head. It was still weird to think about a woman other than my wife that way. I'd been on a few dates in the four years since losing Allison, but nothing stuck. Grace was the first person to spark my interest.

I wasn't sure why I felt like Grace might be that person, especially since I barely knew her, and she clearly wanted nothing to do with me.

"Daddy!" Abby called excitedly.

"Abs!" I replied, equally as excited.

"That lady wrote this book!" she said, holding up a hardcover children's book with a colorful illustration on the cover.

"Really?" I said, taking the book from my daughter and eyeing it speculatively. "Are you sure?"

Abby giggled. "Yes, Daddy. Can I get one? She'll even put her autograph in it!" We'd gone to DisneyLand over the summer--an effort to cheer Abby up--and Abby was most excited about getting all the characters to sign her little autograph book. She didn't go on a single ride, just ran around the park looking for characters.

"Of course, you can, baby girl."

I paid the author's assistant $30--I'm clearly in the wrong business--for the book and my daughter happily spelled out her name to the lady who had been reading to the kids a few minutes ago.

We left the library hand-in-hand, with a promise to come back next weekend to check out a new book.

I saw Grace in the grocery store later that night.

I'd left Abby with my parents for a little while so I could get some grocery shopping done. I could have taken her with me...if I wanted an additional three grocery bags full of sugary garbage. Doing the shopping solo was the only way I could leave the store with all the food groups and not break my budget.

"I'm not sure which one of us got here first, so I'm not sure who is stalking who."

"Whom," she said, not taking her eyes off the yogurt display. She smelled like strawberries, which was also the flavor she grabbed off the shelf.

"Huh?"

"Who is stalking whom."

"Sure," I said. "Whatever you say."

She took a few more containers off the shelf and put them in her basket, then walked away.

"You're giving me a complex, Grace." I said, and she stopped in her tracks at the sound of her name.

"What do you want?" she asked, turning cautiously to me.

"Just to talk. To say hello. I don't know. Why are you being so rude?"

She scoffed. "I'm guessing you remember me from high school."

"Yeah," I agreed. I remembered her now, though it was still difficult to reconcile adult Grace with high school Grace.

"Then you should know that I have every reason to be evasive. Every reason to be skeptical of why any of the *chosen ones* would want to speak to me."

"Chosen ones?" Is that what we were called? I had been popular, but I wasn't an asshole about it like some of my friends were. Like Rosanna, for example. In retrospect, I still didn't know what I'd seen in that girl.

Grace rolled her eyes. "I don't have time to talk." She turned around and began to walk away again.

"Wait, Grace." She sighed but turned around. "There's a fundraiser for the Gaston Library."

"Yeah."

"Go with me."

She laughed. She actually laughed in my face. "No," she said simply. Then she was gone.

What the hell was that, Jonah? I asked myself. I hadn't been planning to ask her to the fundraiser, but I panicked. I needed her attention for one more minute and *that's* what came out of my mouth. I could practically hear Allison laughing at me. "That's the best you could do?" she'd ask. I was much smoother when I'd met Allison in college.

Funny thing was...she'd said no to me, too.

Chapter 7
Grace

The audacity of that man. Asking me to the fundraiser. I'd already planned on going to the event because the cause was near and dear to my heart. But I wasn't going to go with a date. I didn't need a date. I hadn't needed one for prom, I didn't need one for the fundraiser.

We all know how prom went for you, a little niggling voice said, *maybe you could use a date.*

"Shut up," I said.

"Huh?"

I looked down at the student standing across the desk. *Shit.* When had he gotten there?

"Sorry, I was thinking out loud. Need to shut this drawer," I said, closing the drawer that was mercifully left open beside me.

The boy looked at me like I was crazy, which I probably was. He left quickly after I checked out his books. I was sure he'd go tell his friends about the nutty librarian. Oh well, I'd dealt with worse than a few elementary school kids.

I picked up a small pile of books that had been returned during the last hour and wandered off into the stacks to reshelf them. The school day was almost over, and it had been a long one. The entire week had been long, particularly since I spent most of it dodging Jonah Bell. I didn't believe he was stalking me; it was just one of the hazards of living in a small town. Want to go out to dinner? A third of the town will be at one restaurant, another third at the other, and the rest were eating at home. Need coffee in the morning? Gas? So does everyone else. I'd ducked behind more shelves, people, and merchandise displays than I cared to admit. All because he asked me on a date to the fundraiser.

The final bell rang, letting students know it was time to pack up for the end of the day. I finished shelving returns and then spent a few minutes straightening the displays and then my desk. Just as I was reviewing my agenda for Monday, the library doors swung open. I looked up to see Nannette, the receptionist from the front office.

"What can I do for you, Nan?" I asked.

"Well, it seems this young lady is looking for you." She stepped to the side and revealed Abigail Bell standing behind her.

I walked around the desk and crouched down in front of Abby. "Why aren't you waiting outside for your dad?" I'd seen her and Jonah walking home from school a few times, so I knew that was their routine.

"He's running late," Abby said.

"He called in, and Miss Abigail has been sitting in the office with me, but she asked if she could come to the library instead. Said she needed to talk to the library princess."

"Princess Librarian," Abby corrected.

I smiled at the sweet girl. "You can wait here for your dad," I told Abby, and she smiled from ear to ear. "Is that alright with you, Nannette?"

"Sure," Nannette said. "As long as it's not too much trouble for you."

"No trouble at all," I assured her. I had been wanting to go home, but I could spare some time for Abby. "Just give me a call when Mr. Bell arrives, and I'll send her down."

Nannette nodded, and with a light pat to Abby's shoulder she left the library.

"So, what would you like to do?" I asked Abby.

"When I was here with my class this week, there were a few books I wanted to check out, but I had to choose only one. I want to read the others, too."

Mrs. Murphy's rule was stupid. Why put a limit on a child's reading? We should be fostering their desire to read, not hampering it.

"Go ahead," I said, scooting her to the children's section. Each class was allowed thirty minutes to browse during their assigned time and Mrs. Murphy gave her class maybe half of that. I should report her to the administration. It wasn't right. Unfortunately, the arts tended to rank low on most administrators' priority lists, so my efforts probably would have been futile.

I returned to my computer and started working on a flyer for an upcoming book fair that had been on my agenda for Monday since I had nothing else to organize or clean while Abby waited for her dad.

Twenty minutes passed, and I wondered just how late Jonah was going to be. I adjusted my glasses--I needed them when working on the computer--and continued to work on the flyer. The previous librarian had told me that the school book fairs weren't well attended by the students and parents. I planned to change that, and this flyer was the first step. When I was finished, I planned to speak with the principal, Jefferson Lawrence, about developing a way to incentivize participation. A simple token economy could be an effective and inexpensive way to get kids interested in reading. It might also solve the problem with Mrs. Murphy's class. The next item on my agenda was to work on a pitch for the token economy.

"You're really pretty when you're concentrating."

"Jesus!" I jumped, knocking over my pencil cup and sending pens and pencils across my desk. "Can you ever just announce yourself like a normal person?" I asked, my breath heavy. "You scared the hell out of me."

"Sorry, I've been standing in the doorway for a few minutes. I thought the squeak would have alerted you to my presence."

"I'm used to the damn squeak," I said. The first few days of school it had driven me crazy, but now I didn't even hear it.

"Sorry," he said again. He picked up a pencil off the floor and placed it in the cup.

"I've got it," I barked at him. "Abby is in the back," I said, gesturing with my chin to the aisle she'd disappeared down as I placed the pens and pencils back in the cup.

"Thanks for letting her spend some time here. She loves to read and spending time in the library is probably like paradise to her. I'm sorry I was so late..."

He trailed off as I refused to look at him, still placing each writing utensil back in the cup, one at a time. Anything to occupy my time until he left again. I would not give him the opportunity to ask me on a date again.

"I don't know why you hate me so much," he finally said. I scoffed, *whatever*. "I always liked you in high school." His words caught my attention, but I still wouldn't look at him. "*Liked* isn't the right word...I *admired* you."

My eyes shot up to his. "You what?"

"I admired you, Grace. We went to school with a bunch of idiots. The things they said to you...did to you. It wasn't right. You handled it all with such grace, though. Like you didn't care at all. It drove them crazy, I'll tell you that. Your lack of reaction to their taunts made them insane. Looking back, I'm ashamed I was even friends with some of them."

I looked at him in shock. He'd admired me? He thought I'd handled my bullies with grace? He thought I drove them crazy? I felt dizzy with this information...disoriented even. Was that why they'd pulled the ultimate prank on me at prom? Because I'd pissed them off by not reacting to their barbs?

"That's why I want to talk to you. That's why I'm trying to be your friend. I don't know many people around here anymore. In fact, I have no friends in town at all. Plus, Abby likes you, so you've got to be good people. When I saw you in the old room at the library, you had this look of utter peace on your face. I thought the fundraiser would be a way for us to hang out and maybe get to know one another. That's all. I just want to get to know you, Grace. I don't have ill intentions, okay?"

I didn't know what to say. My mouth was dry, and my heart thudded in my chest. Bump. Bump. Bump. I stood there looking at him but not really seeing him.

"I'd better get Abs and head home. I'm sorry for bothering you. I won't do it anymore, if that's what you want."

Jonah walked down the aisle I'd gestured to and came back a minute later with Abby.

"I put the books back where I got them, Miss Grace," Abby told me.

Realizing I had to respond to her, I smiled. "I didn't doubt you would." I hadn't told her my name, so I'd bet Jonah did. Hearing her small, sweet voice say my name melted my heart a little bit.

"Say good night, Abs," Jonah said.

"Good night, Miss Grace. Thanks for letting me stay."

"Good night, Abby. You are welcome any time."

She beamed up at me, before walking through the door Jonah was holding open for her.

"I'll go with you," I called out, surprising myself as much as I surprised Jonah. "To the fundraiser. I'll go with you."

He smiled and nodded, then left. *That smile!* It sent tingles throughout my entire body.

I groaned, collapsing across my desk.

What was I getting myself into?

I could very easily fall for those two, and I wasn't sure just how hard I'd land.

Chapter 8
Grace

I'd had to go about twenty miles past Gaston to Charming to find a costume shop that had the appropriate period attire for the historical themed fundraiser. Really, any decade would have been fine. There were ladies dressed like they'd walked off the set of *The Great Gatsby* and men competing to be the next James Dean. Most of the decades were represented, but I'd gone for another century altogether.

I wore an antique gown made of a heavy, blush fabric. There was cream colored lacing on the bodice and around the neckline. Creamy lace sleeves flowed down to my wrists. My hair was pulled back into a loose ponytail, my long curls mostly draping down my back.

The best part of the costume?

Jonah matched me.

He wore a suit made from a similar fabric, only a darker shade of blush. There was cream thread embroidered throughout the velour fabric. The laced ends of the shirt he wore came out from beneath his jacket sleeves. He wore his long hair down, and he looked wild and sexy.

Together, we looked like we'd stepped right off the set of *Interview with a Vampire*. It hadn't

43

been the look I was going for, but it was perfect in its own way.

I'd let him bite me; my cheeks heated at the thought.

We'd met at the event. While he had melted some of my shell with his speech in my library, I wasn't quite ready for him to pick me up at home. I wasn't ready for my mother to ask questions and I wasn't ready for this to be more of a date than it already was. Until recently, I'd thought Jonah--J.T.--had been my nemesis.

I wasn't sure how I felt about this new development...after believing something that wasn't true for so long.

He said he'd always wanted to be my friend in high school, and I'd always wanted to be his...something...too. What if we'd actually done something about it back then? What if we'd talked? What if we'd been friends? Would we still be friends now? If he'd wanted to talk to me back then, why hadn't he? I had so many questions.

"What's going on in there?" Jonah asked, sending one of his sexy smiles my way. I flushed, feeling like I was caught thinking about him. He couldn't possibly know what was going on in my head, but it probably showed on my face. We stood side-by-side along the perimeter of the room. We'd made our way around when we arrived, looking at the various exhibits from the library and bidding on a few silent auction items. I had my heart set on a three-day trip to Disney, but I'd probably be outbid before the night was through. The organizers boasted that ninety-five percent of all donations would go towards the renovation of the preservation room and the acquisition of new volumes. I hadn't personally made it through all the books in the room yet, but the thought of new books still excited me.

"I'm sorry, just lost in thought about books," I said, smiling shyly. It wasn't entirely a lie; I had been thinking about the books a little bit.

"Hazard of the job?" He asked, and I nodded. "Would you like something to drink? It looks like they're passing around champagne."

"I'd love some," I said. I didn't like champagne that much, but I could sip it for a little while.

Jonah took two champagne flutes off a passing tray and handed one to me. "To new friends," he said, holding the glass up to me.

I smiled. "To new friends," I said, clinking my glass against his. I took a sip, the bitter taste causing me to wince.

He let out an amused laugh. "You don't like champagne?"

"Is it that obvious?" I laughed softly.

He took the flute from me and placed it on the empty tray of another passing server. "They have a punch bowl set up over there, I'll go get you something. Then we can dance."

I gawked as he walked away. *He wanted to dance?* I had two left feet. Dancing was not going to end well.

"If it isn't Leatherface," someone said, and the blood drained from my face. After ten years, I still recognized that voice. I'd never forget it.

I turned and looked directly into Rosanna's eyes. She was still as pretty as she'd been in high school. Petite with glowing skin and sparkly white teeth that shone beneath her sneer. She was one of the Gatsby flappers with a gold sequin dress hugged tightly to her slim figure.

Figures she'd still be beautiful...and ugly at the same time.

"You look good," she said, eyeing me up and down.

My jaw hurt from clenching it so tightly. I didn't know what she wanted with me, but high school was over a long time ago. Surely, she had better things to do.

She was looking at something--someone--across the room. I followed her gaze. "I couldn't believe it when he told me he was taking you to the event. I told him it was cruel, but he didn't care."

That dizzying feeling was back, made worse by the corset I had to wear to properly fit into my dress. I tried to take a deep breath, but I couldn't. It was like something was pressing against my chest. The music seemed to quiet and suddenly all I could hear was Rosanna in the big room.

"He was always interested in the charity cases. That's all you are to him, Grace. A charity case. First when you were Scarface, and now as the nerdy librarian at the elementary school."

She kept talking, but I stopped hearing her.

I wouldn't cry. Not this time. I wasn't even upset.

I was angry.

I was spitting mad.

Blinded by my anger, I took a few steps towards Jonah as he approached me, smiling with our drinks.

I shoved him.

The drinks fell to the floor, splashing at our feet. The clear plastic cups bounced and rolled away. Jonah looked shocked; his eyes wide. When he looked past me, his eyes narrowed at Rosanna.

I didn't care that he seemed angry to see her. I ignored him altogether.

I turned and walked out of the gym.

Out of the school.

With my head held high this time.

I knew it was too good to be true.

I couldn't trust him...I couldn't trust anyone.

Chapter 9
Jonah

"What did you say to her?" I spit, getting right in Rosanna's face. She had been a narcissistic bitch in high school, and it was evident that hadn't changed.

She shrugged, a smirk spreading across her face. "Nothing she didn't already know."

"Why are you such a bitch?"

Her smile froze and she looked around us to see if anyone was within earshot. A few people were. "Jonah," she said, smiling awkwardly at the onlookers.

"We are not friends, Rosanna. We haven't been friends for years. To be honest, I don't know why I considered you a friend back then. You are not a nice person. I don't know what you said to Grace, but you should be ashamed of yourself. You're a grown woman, stop being a bully."

"Jonah," she called. "Jonah, wait."

I heard the clack clack clack of her heels on the gym floor as she followed behind me, but I didn't stop. I needed to find Grace before Rosanna did more damage than she'd done at our senior prom.

"Grace," I called, throwing a pebble at what I guessed was her bedroom window. I'd had to ask around town to find out where she lived and almost two hours had passed since she left the event. Turned out she was on the next block over from me, staying at her mother's place because she was sick. Grace was a saint, all the more reason she didn't deserve whatever Rosanna said.

"Young man," someone called, and I turned towards the voice. It was a woman who must have been Grace's mother since she looked so much like her. She looked tired through, and she wore a pink bandana around her head.

"I'm sorry, ma'am," I said. "I'm looking for Grace."

"She's not here," she said.

"Oh." My shoulders sagged in defeat.

"She went for ice cream. She should be back any minute."

I let out a breath. "Thank you, Mrs. Adams."

"It's *Ms.* Adams, and don't make me regret it. Grace has had a little pep in her step the past week and I can only assume you put it there."

I smiled, knowing I'd made her happy despite how standoffish she'd been. "I don't want to hurt her, Ms. Adams."

She nodded. "Good." She went back into the house, and I leaned against my car, waiting for Grace to return.

I heard her long sigh before I saw her.

"What are you doing here?" she asked.

I faced her, holding up my hands, my palms facing her in surrender. "Look, I don't know exactly what Rosanna said, but it's bullshit."

"Sure it is," she said, rolling her eyes. "Can you just leave me alone? It's been a long night, and I'm sick and tired of your games."

"I'm not playing any games," I said, taking a step towards her. "I haven't talked to Rosanna since I dumped her on prom night for what she and her friends did to you. I haven't talked to any of them." She looked at me curiously, so I kept going. "I told you I'd always admired you, Grace, and that's the truth. I don't know why I didn't say anything back then. I don't know why I didn't have more courage to stand up against them and tell them to stop bullying you. It seemed like you didn't care, so I guess I just figured you didn't. Maybe I was a coward. But you weren't, Grace. You were amazing. Prom night...when they added the category and edited the slide show...I had no idea. I'd done a run through of everything before prom, so I knew something was off. I was so mad but I was caught off guard, so I made the announcement, anyway. You owned it, though. I was so proud of you when you marched up onto that stage with that beautiful smile on your face. I was so impressed by you in that moment. What happened after that...well I never would have anticipated *that*. I promise I had nothing to do with the water balloons, and I got you out of there as soon as I could."

"Red is so *not* my color," she said after several excruciating seconds, and I exhaled in relief. She was making jokes, so everything was going to be okay, right? "That was you? The one who helped me off the stage?" She took a few steps closer to me.

"You don't remember?" I asked, surprised. I'd talked to her the entire time I helped her out off the stage and out of the cafeteria.

She shook her head. "My eyes were blurry from the dye...and I kind of blocked most of that out, anyway."

"Yeah...it was me. I got you out of there and told the faculty what happened. You never came back to school, but a bunch of the football players got suspended...and Rosanna."

The corner of her mouth lifted slightly. "Good, I'm glad something good came of it." She kicked at a few rocks in the driveway. "It really doesn't change anything, though, Jonah. We're too different."

"What's wrong with being different, Grace? I want to get to know you. I'd like for you to get to know me, too."

She sighed, wrapping her arms around her body, the plastic bag with what I guessed was ice cream hanging from one hand. "There's nothing wrong with being different," she finally said.

"Then give me a chance, Grace. Let's go on a real date."

Her gaze shifted back to me, and her eyes locked with mine for a few silent moments.

"Please," I added, smiling at her and putting my hands together in a praying gesture. I wasn't afraid to beg; I'd be on my knees next.

She blew out another breath. "Okay, fine. I'll go on a date with you."

"Yes," I said, pumping my fist into the air.

"Don't make me regret it, Jonah Bell."

"I won't. I promise."

She shook her head, trying to hide her smile, but I still saw it. I waved as she disappeared inside the house, feeling goofy as hell.

I had a date with Grace Adams, the most beautiful woman in Marchen.

THE END.

Epilogue
Grace

"Where do you want these?" Jonah asked, holding up a few books that had been on my nightstand.

"This box here," I said, pointing to a small box on my bed.

I walked over to the window and looked outside. The sun shone through the trees as a light summer breeze blew, causing shadows to dance across the bright green grass. The rose bushes on the far side of the yard added a vibrant splash of red and pink to the landscape. There were blue skies as far as the eyes could see.

It was a good day to move.

Jonah set the books in the box and came behind me, wrapping his arms around my middle and resting his chin on my shoulder.

"What are you thinking about?" he asked.

My gaze shifted across the yard as I thought of the past year. The highs and the lows. I'd come back to Marchen with very little, and I gained so much.

I turned in his arms and looked up at the man I'd fallen madly in love with.

"I'm thinking about the future," I said. "Our future."

Acknowledgements

I appreciate the opportunity to join the Fractured Fairy Tales Anthology for the 2020 Sexy and Sassy Signing (SaSS). I enjoyed my first SaSS signing so much and hope to be a lifelong SaSSer! Big thanks to my editor, Aimee Lukas, for her friendship, her help when I was stumped, and her work. Thank you to my assistant, Karen, for being there for my whims and for trying to keep me organized. Thank you, Natasha, for being my BFF. Thank you to the Chapter Chicks for being such a cool group of people. Thank you to Brad for always being my number one and for always being there. Thank you to my family for being supportive of this wild side ride I've taken, particularly my Aunt Barbara who passed away at the end of last year. At her funeral services, my cousin told me that every time I released a new book, she'd have him go online to buy it for her. I hope she'll read this one, and I hope she enjoys it. <3 Thanks to the bloggers and anyone else who promotes these stories for us. A big thank you to all the readers who take time out of their day to check this story out, and the ebook anthology! Books would just be a bunch of words if it wasn't for you. Much, much, love to all.

About the Author

Jennifer was born and raised on Long Island, in New York. She relocated to South Carolina in 2002, where she met the love of her life. They got married in 2008, and live their happily ever after just outside of Charleston with their fur-kid. When she's not reading or writing, she works as a behavioral therapist, and is also a graduate student, pursuing a Master Degree in Psychology as well as a Graduate Certificate in Behavior Intervention in Autism. She enjoys amateur photography, traveling, and music...it's a bonus when she can combine all three. Jennifer is also a breast cancer survivor, having been diagnosed in 2017 and declared cancer-free in 2018. She independently published her debut novel, *Our Moon (JACT 1)*, in June 2015.

Connect With Me

Email: jennifer@jenniferlallenauthor.com
Website: www.jenniferlallenauthor.com
Facebook: www.facebook.com/jallenauthor
Mailing List: http://eepurl.com/b4LjgD

Also by Jennifer L. Allen